SALON LIFE

AN URBAN NOVEL

BY

CARLENE BOWMAN

SALON LIFE

CARLENE BOWMAN

Salon Life. Bougie Publication. All rights reserved. ©

Warning: The unauthorized reproduction or distribution of this copyrighted work is illegal. Criminal copyright infringement, including infringement without monetary gain, is investigated by the FBI and is punishable by up to five (5) years in federal prison and a fine of $250,000.

No part of this book may be reproduced or transmitted in any form or by any means, electronic or mechanical, including photocopying, recording, or by any information storage and retrieval system, without permission in writing from the publisher.

Salon Life 1st EBook Edition June 2015 ©

Written by Carlene Bowman

ACKNOWLEDGEMENTS

First and foremost, I'd like to thank God for seeing me through this amazing journey. I put all trust in him and give Him all the praise.

To my greatest creation, Shaylene: I love you with all my heart!!

To my Mother: thank you for your input and your support. Without you, there would be no me. I love you with all my heart.

To Willie A. Bowman, my father: I know you're looking down saying, *"That's my girl. I knew you could do it. It was a struggle, but yes, you did it!* If you were here, I'd give you the biggest hug. But, I know you're smiling and looking down, sharing this moment with me.

Shirley Johnson Taylor: thanks for having my back and being my biggest supporter. Without you I don't know what I do. I Love you.

Lisa North: thanks for being my biggest supporter. You always keep it real, never sugar coating nothing. Love you to death and thank you so much!!!!! I appreciate you!!

Greg Peete: thank you so much for the blessing you've given me.

Latonya King my mentor: thanks for teaching me all you could, and for supporting me through anything I've done. You're always just a phone call away. I thank you and love you.

Thank you Platinum Hair Gallery Family: Gwen, Shanetta, Eboni, Tasha, and Mary; you all are the best. You all helped me so much and I appreciate all of you. Thank you!!!

Mr. Melvin Ward: thank you for giving me that extra push, and for keeping it real, giving it to me straight, no chaser. Most of all, thank you for being an ear and one of my supporters. You are truly a friend. Thank you.

Stephanie Johnson you jumped right in from day one and always had my back. You were one of my mentors. I don't think you even knew it. I appreciate all you've done for me. Thank you

My Four Stars and Black Radiance Family, where it all started.... I love you all!!!

Thank you, Eric Calles, Deonica Henderson, and Latarsha Dutch for all of your support. I appreciate you and Thank you

Mrs. Dorothy Edwards, you taught me all about the business. You always would say little money make big money. I live by that to this day. I know you're looking down saying, *"I knew she could do it!"* while smiling and rubbing your legs. You were one of the best that ever did it! Thank you may you rest in peace.

Special thanks to my stylist, Mozella Malone, you rock.

Cook E. Portraits: thanks for capturing my vision, you're the best.

My graphic artist, Jermaine Juju Edwards, your work is amazing! Thank you for making my work come to life, you are the best!!

Cassandra Sim, thank you so much!! You taught me more than you will ever know!! Girl, you Rock!! I appreciate you!!!!

Thank you to everyone for your support!!

~ *Author Carlene Bowman* ~

CHAPTER 1

WELCOME TO MY WORLD

Let me introduce myself. My name is Star. I wasn't born with this name; it was given to me because of my talent.

Once I had mastered my craft you couldn't tell me nothing! Instead, I let my work speak for itself. After you've seen my work for yourselves you'll truly understand why they call me Star.

My clientele is off da chain. I get my clients thru referrals and appointments only. They come from near and far just to get a chance to sit in my chair. That's right. I'm the *crème da la crème.* You can even fly me in, just make sure my flight is first class and make sure my accommodations are five-star.

I get car service wherever I go. I'm the one who makes sure the ladies are looking fierce enough to walk the Red Carpet. I'm the best that ever did it. The Bitches be hatin' and the men be trippin'. I walk it and I talk it, but becoming Star wasn't easy, and being Karlissa was even harder.

Karlissa is my government name. You know........the name on your birth certificate? I always hated that name. No one could pronounce Karlissa and I always wanted to change it, but my mother wouldn't let me. Most people called me Lissa, except my Mother; she called me Karlee.

Momma D was laid back. As long as you got good grades and did your chores you could do what you pleased. But, if she told you to do something, you had better damn well do it, and in a hurry! She'd knock the shit out of you if you didn't. There were only three of us. I was the oldest so I was allowed to do more. Growing up I had to set the example for my brother and sister. Humph, boy did that go out the window fast!

I always loved to do hair. I would always have people lined up in my living room waiting to get their hair done. One day Momma D came home from work just cussin' and fussin'.

"Karlee why are all these damn people in my house?" she asked.

"Ma, I had clients today and I just got a little behind, that's all," I answered.

"I see, but you better get all that damn hair up and you better not break my vacuum cleaner doin' it either. Better yet, sweep it up then you won't have that problem," she added in sarcastically.

"Ma, it's faster with the vacuum cleaner," I pouted.

"What did I say?" She raised her voice.

"Okay! Mess around and break my damn vacuum cleaner yo' ass gonna be in the store gettin' me a new one!"

"Okay, Ma. I'll sweep," I replied, agreeing with her.

"I thought you'd see it my way."

"Ma," I shouted.

"Girl, stop calling my name.

"Ma......," I said in a voice that let her know I was up to something.

"What is it, Karlee?" she asked in a curious tone.

"Can I go to hair school or take a few cosmetology classes while I'm in high school?"

"No, girl, you goin' to college and get yourself a degree."

Her answer didn't really surprise me because she'd always been big on education. I at least thought she'd hear me out before giving me such a final answer.

"But, Ma," I whined.

"But, Ma, nothin', you better keep doin' hair as a hobby, and in the meantime, get your degree, girl. Once you get a job then you can pay your own way thru beauty school," she said giving me her usual motherly advice.

"Ma, I wanna go to beauty school and get my license."

"Yep, you sure can get your license with the money you make after you get your degree," she said, still not in total agreement.

"Okay, but I'm going one way or another; I love doin' hair, Ma."

"Well, I don't know about all that, Karlee. But, what you can do is get these people out of my house! That's what you *can* do," she said.

I knew now wasn't the best time to really talk about it, so, I decided to let it go… for now. "Can you at least think about it, Ma? Pretty please," I begged.

"Karlee, you're pressin' your luck, young lady. And where's your brother?" she asked. When she changed the subject without answering me the last time, I knew she'd momentarily made up her mind.

Oh well, I'm still not giving up, I thought to myself before replying to my mother. "I ain't seen him today. He's probably foolin' around with his friends since he ain't come in from school yet."

"Ain't it almost six clock?" she asked.

"Yeah, it is, Ma."

"Well, where's your sister?" She continued probing me about the whereabouts of my siblings.

"She's sleep, Ma," I answered. What I really wanted to say was *I could care less where they are! I wanna know why you won't agree to let me go to hair school!*

"Sleep?"

"Yeah, Ma, she's sleep," I informed her a second time. This time it was hard for to hide the irritation in my voice, but I knew better than to get smart with my mother. Besides, I knew she wouldn't stop with the questions until I'd given her all the 411 on my brother and sister. So, I filled her in. "She came in, did her chores, did her homework and took a nap."

"I done told her lazy ass about that. Now, she *think* she gonna be on that damn phone all night. Humph," my mother added. "She got another *thing* comin!"

Oh, no, Momma D didn't play that! Whatever she said, you better damn sho' believe she meant every word of it. She knew my sister's routine better than me. And, if there's one thing my sister loved, it was the telephone. She'd sleep all afternoon and then wanna hog the phone all night, for hours at a time.

I guess mama gonna burst her bubble tonight, I thought to myself as I laughed out loud.

CHAPTER 2

KARLEE

I made a promise to myself that I was going to hair school even if I had to pay for it myself. Eventually, my plans worked out perfect, all except for one thing .... Kayla.

Kayla is my world, the reason my heart beats; she's my daughter. I got pregnant while attending college. I always went to class but I'd also stayed at *The GoGo*.

Kayla's father never had a problem with me partying. He never tried to change me. Deon was just a cool guy. Now, if truth be told, that cool guy also came with couple of problems. He was fourteen years older than me and on house arrest. Hell, he had actually committed the crime the day I was born. So, while I was walking across the stage to get my High School diploma, he was getting handcuffed and dragged off to Lorton to serve two years in jail.

Unfortunately, he was on house arrest for the first six months of my pregnancy. So that, in and of itself, made it easy to hide our relationship from Momma D. To say, I had hated him through my entire pregnancy would've been an understatement. I knew the day would come when Deon would have to meet my family, but I never imagined it to be like this.

Once Kayla was born, everything changed and it was all about her.

My father didn't know I had company over that particular day, and he had taken one look at Deon and started screaming my name.

"Karlee!" he yelled in a harsh tone, "Karlee!"

"Yes, Daddy," I replied. "Why are you yelling my name like that?" I asked.

"Is this that the baby's father? She looks just like him," my dad said, as he studied Deon's facial features. "So, that's why she's so chocolate," he added in reference to my baby's skin complexion, "I thought it was because of me."

"I don't know why you thought it was 'cause of you, Daddy," she said in a disagreeing tone.

"Shit, look how black I am, that baby just as black as me," he said in a funny but sarcastic manner.

"Well, I'm sorry to inform you, but no her complexion has nothing to do with you....actually, she gets it from her father Deon."

When Momma D walked in and saw they had company, she looked over at Deon, extending her hand. "Hello, baby, my name is Darla," she said with a smile on her face.

Deon turned his stare towards her before speaking. "Oh hey, Darla, nice to meet you, I'm Deon."

"I see you've met Randy," Darla said. She had noticed the two of them conversing before she interrupted.

"Yes, I've met Randy," Deon confirmed.

At that moment, Randy looked backed over at Deon, as if he were in deep thought. "Deon, if you don't mind me asking, how old are you while snatching Deon's hat off?" he asked curiously.

Karlee hated when he did that so she quickly butted in. "Daddy, please don't start! Give the man his hat back, and please, go back upstairs! My God, you so nosey!" she added in an irritated tone.

"Nah, I ain't tryna be nosey. I'm just saying....I know he's not no spring chicken, is all," he said followed by a light chuckle.

"He looks about your age, Randy," Darla said, adding her two cents, "but, even if he is, it's none of your business. "Let's go," she said pointing her index finger towards the stairs as if he were a child, "and let him visit Karlee in peace."

Ever since that day it's been all about Kayla. He did everything for Kayla, and all I had to do was take care of her. He took her to the doctors and made sure she got to the babysitter's. She was his world. Not a day would go by that he didn't spend time with her or buy her something, just because. She was his heart.

Momma D had noticed everything Deon had been doing for Kayla. She didn't play when it came to her kids, and now that she had a grandbaby she really didn't play when it came to her.

Yep, it was time to sink or swim, and being that I loved Deon, I hoped he wouldn't drown.

****

My mom walked in the room where I was sitting, waiting on Deon to arrive. I knew her so well, and by the look she wore on her face, I knew she was there to interrogate me further.

Without so much as a hello, just like I knew she would, she started in on me. "Karlee, can we talk a minute before Deon gets here?"

"Yea, sure, Ma. Is something wrong?" I asked, hoping it wouldn't be as bad I thought.

"No, nothing is wrong, baby. Well, nothing that can't be fixed," she added. "Have a seat."

I moved over closer to where my mom was seated to let her know I was listening. "Okay, Ma, what's wrong, tell me," I said.

"Well, Karlee," she said and paused…. "I think it's time for you and Deon to get a place of your own."

"But, Ma," I started in a whiney voice. I'd always use that tone with my mother when I wanted her to see things my way. "I can't afford to pay rent without a job. Besides that," I added, "I haven't even finished school yet."

"I know, baby," she said acknowledging her understanding, "but you've started a family, and Deon should be able to provide a home for you and your daughter, Kayla."

"Ma, Deon doesn't even have his own place yet. If he did, I'm sure he'd invite me and Kayla to live with him as a family," I said.

"I know that, Karlee," she agreed. "All I'm saying is, it's time for y'all to grow up. Deon is too old not to have his own place. Always remember, God blesses the child who has his own."

"What does that mean, Ma?" I asked not fully understanding.

"What it means is, always make sure you have a roof over yours and Kayla's head. If you don't pay nothin' else, pay your rent and your babysitter; they go hand and hand. If you don't have nothin' else you'll at least have a place to live. If the two of you do happen to get a place together, just make sure your name is on the lease too. That way, he can never put you out."

"How soon do I have before I have to move, Ma?" I asked, knowing she wouldn't just put me out on the streets.

"I'll give you couple of months, Karlee," she answered.

"What if I move and it doesn't work out, can I come back?" I asked. Just the thought of living on my own, and with a child had me nervous.

"Yes, baby, you'll always have a home to come back to," she said in a motherly tone. I knew she meant it sincerely. "All you can do is try, baby, and do what's right by your child. Nothing beats a failure but a try," she added in.

"I promise to try my hardest, Ma," I assured her, "it's just so sudden." I was almost on the verge of tears, but as I held them back, I knew in my heart, it was time for me to grow up.

"But, it's time Karlee. Baby, it's time. You're a mother yourself now, with a child of your own. Being a mother comes with great responsibility," she said, speaking from her own experience.

"Well let me get dressed, Ma. Thanks for the talk," I said, ending our conversation, "Deon will be here any minute."

Okay, baby, enjoy yourself. Make sure you wrap Kayla up good when you take her out," she said, before turning to walk away.

****

Damn, I thought to myself as I waited on Deon. *My mom is really putting me out, how am I gonna tell Deon. He's gonna have a fit, I just know he is. Oh well, she's right, it is time. I'm twenty years old and I do need more space. Kayla will be turning a year old in three months, and s*he*'ll need her own bed and space. Besides, I'm ready for the next chapter in life,* I pondered. *Like mom said, nothing beats a failure but a try.*

Bringing me out of my thoughts, I heard Deon shouting my name, loudly.

"Dang, Deon, you so loud," I said when he entered.

"Hey Kayla, *Baby Mama!*" he said. Referring to me as *"Baby Mama"* was an inside joke between the two of us, and I couldn't help from laughing out loud.

"Ha, ha," I said, still laughing, "funny! But, guess what?"

He looked at me with a weird expression on his face, as if he were contemplating on if he really wanted to know what it was I had to tell him. Finally, he replied with, "What?"

"My momma told me it was time for me to move out," I blurted out without hesitation.

"How you gonna do that? You don't have a job yet."

Well, duh, I thought to myself, *tell me something I don't know,* I wanted to say. But instead, I simply replied and said, "I know. I guess I'll have to use my check. I was hoping you would help me out too," I threw in quickly.

"Lissa," he started, cutting my name in half, "I don't have a job either, or a place to stay. Not only that, but I'm still on house arrest. You do remember that, don't you?"

"Yes, I know, Deon. So what? Are you saying *no*, you *won't* help me?" I asked in a surprised tone. I mean, I knew all he'd stated was true. But, I also at least expected him to say he'd try, or do the best he could. After all, Kayla wasn't just my daughter; she was just as much his responsibility as she was mine.

"Exactly, that's what I'm saying! I can't help you if I have nothing to help you with, Lissa!" I guess he noticed the frown on my face because he suddenly switched it up. "Well, I can help when I can," he finally said, "I'll always do my part with Kayla."

For the moment, I would accept his response. The truth of the matter was, what other choice did I have? "Okay cool," I said in agreement.

After that day, I never looked at Deon the same. He was just Kayla's father, and he had let me know I had to make it on my own. That's when the job hunting began.....

****

I Knew College wasn't for me 'cause I kept falling asleep in class. It didn't help any that I'd party almost every day of the week. At the time, I was also pregnant with Kayla. I wasn't able to keep my internship and go to beauty school, so I resigned and applied for hair school. It helped the time pass by while I was pregnant and it also kept me busy. I went on maternity leave, and it ended up lasting for an entire a year.

Now, it was time to go back and get my license.

While attending school I was able to work as a shampoo assistant in a salon. I decided to try my luck and start calling around to different salons, on a hunt for a job. I called at least twenty salons, and no one needed a shampoo assistant.

I was ready to give up, but in my heart, I knew giving up was unacceptable; not only that, I needed income to provide for me and my daughter, Kayla.

"Hello is the owner or the manager in?" I asked.

"Yes, may I ask whose calling?" the person who answered had asked.

"Yes, my name is Karlissa," I responded in my best professional voice.

"Hi, Karlissa, my name is Sonya. How may I help you?" she asked.

"Hi, Sonya," I said into the receiver, "I was calling too see if you had any openings for a shampoo assistant?" I asked, with fingers crossed.

"Yes, I do. Actually," she said, "I need someone ASAP. Are you in school?" she inquired.

"Yes. I have classes from 8am to 12 noon."

"Those are perfect hours," she answered, "I start my bookings at 12pm. Can you come to the salon to be interviewed?" she asked as I smiled on the other end.

"I sure can! I can be there within the hour," I said happily.

"Okay, see you then," she said, ending the call.

Yes, finally! I thought to myself. Now, let me hurry up before she changes her mind. I better ask Momma D to watch Kayla while I go.

"Ma," I yelled. "Can you watch Kayla? I got an interview at a salon."

"Sure Karlee," she said without hesitation, "see you when you get back and good luck."

"Thanks Ma! Bye Kayla!" I shouted, as I headed out the door.

Dang, I am so scared but I need this job. I hope she's cool people. She seemed cool on the phone. Just gotta keep it business and not personal. I guess this is it. I thought the whole way there.

"Hello I'm here to see Sonya," I said after I walked in.

"Hello, I'm Sonya. Do you have an appointment?" she asked.

"No, I mean yeah!" I answered and chuckled lightly. My nerves were all over the place and I guess Sonya could tell. "No, I meant, I'm Karlissa, Sonya. I called about being a shampoo assistant," I finally managed to get out.

"Ok, you got here fast," she replied.

"Yes, I don't stay too far from here."

"Well, follow me and let's sit down, so we can get to know one another," she suggested.

"Okay cool," I agreed.

"How much time do you have left before you finish school, Karlissa?"

"About six more months, not long at all," I answered.

"What are your plans afterwards?" she probed.

"I plan to become a stylist and work in a salon," I answered quickly. Although my answers flowed more freely than they had when I'd first arrived, in my mind, I still prayed I was making a good first-impression. I needed this job in the worst way.

"Well, Karlissa you're doing the right thing by becoming an assistant first. It will give you hands-on training," she said.

"That's what I need. I do hair at home but I know there's so much more I need to learn," I replied honestly.

"You will in time," she said. Her tone was encouraging, and I knew I'd landed the job when she looked at me, smiled and said, "I like you Karlissa."

"You can call me Lissa, everyone does," I offered, my tone friendly.

"If that's what you prefer, then okay, Lissa it is. How soon can you start, Lissa?" she asked with a smile on her face.

"I'm available whenever you need me to start," I asked. I was so excited I was tempted to ask could I stay and start right away.

"I forgot to ask. Do you have any kids?" she asked becoming more personal.

"Yes, a daughter. Is that a problem?" I countered. Now, I was worried she'd change her mind.

Instead she said, "Oh, great! I have a son, as a matter of fact, there he is right there," she said, pointing towards a little boy. "Boy, get your ass down now!" she yelled, before turning her attention back towards me. "Sorry for that," she added.

"It's okay, kids will be kids," I said as I laughed.

"That's what you have to look forward to, I hope you're ready," she replied.

"*I have no choice.*"

"*Come on, girl, let me show you around,*" *she offered as she led the way.*

Sonya showed me around, as I got to know everyone in the salon.

****

After being there for a couple of months Sonya and I became the best of friends. Sonya became Kayla's Godmother and she always looked out for us. She taught me so much while I was her assistant, and she played a big part in my life.

Momma D was my babysitter. Every time I got ready to leave Kayla it was always something; either she wasn't there or she just flat out said *I ain't watchin' her today.* I'd end up missing work or calling Deon to come get Kayla. Sonya ended up picking me and Kayla up a many of time.

But, the last time had been after a bad snow storm. Momma D was like....*I hope Kayla's going with you 'cause I ain't watchin' nobody's child today!* I had to call Sonya and tell her I couldn't come in because I didn't have anyone to watch Kayla. Sonya was pissed that day...

"Lissa, I'm about to come get y'all so be ready," she said.

I hurried to get our stuff together when Sonya pulled up.

"Hey, Sonya, thank you," I said as soon as I got in her car.

"No problem," she replied back. "Look, it's okay to bring her to work with you every day, she's no problem."

"Okay," I said.

"What about Deon's mom? Why don't you see if she can babysit for you while you work?" she asked.

"I don't know, Sonya," I answered solemnly.

"Just ask," she said.

"I will. Deon always says let her go to my mother's daycare. I'll have to soon though or I won't have a job. I can't let that happen or I'll end homeless," I replied again.

"Exactly, Lissa," Sonya agreed, "so get to asking. Here, call Deon now," she said as she offered me her cell phone.

"Alright," I answered reluctantly. I dialed his number and waited for him to answer. "Hey Deon," I greeted after he'd picked up.

"What's up baby momma?" he asked like always.

"Ugh! Why do you always have to say that?" I asked in an irritated tone.

"Because, you're my baby momma," he said and laughed out loud.

"You so ghetto," I replied. "Look, can you ask your mother if Kayla can come to her daycare and how much it'll cost?" I asked, getting straight to the point. "Oh and when can I come and see it?" I added.

"What Lissa? What happened now with Momma D?" he asked. He knew how my momma was and he knew her moods changed like the weather.

"Well, I started, "I got up today and she was like…. *take her with you.*"

"What?" He asked in a baffled tone, "You mean to tell me, it's cold as I don't know what and she made you take Kayla with you?"

"Yes, Sonya came and got us," I explained.

"Lissa, you gotta hurry up and find a place. She doing it out of spite," he said. "You better not take my baby on the bus in this damn cold ass weather. Better yet, I'll pick her up in the mornings and drop her off in evenings," he offered.

"Sounds good to me," I said, relieved at his suggestion.

"Thanks Deon."

"Whatever, now you got my blood boiling!" he said in angry voice.

"Calm down! It ain't that serious, Deon," I urged him.

"Lissa! Maybe not to you but to me that's unacceptable."

"Bye Deon," I said, "let it go for now. At least we got a plan and everything gonna work itself out."

"I'll be over there in a little while," he added in.

"For what?" I asked.

"Lissa, don't play with me! I wanna see y'all."

"Yeah, okay talk to you later!"

"Bye, baby mamma," he said before ending the call.

"See…..was that so hard?" Sonya asked after overhearing our conversation.

"No, I guess not," I said, feeling better already. "Let's just hope it works, Sonya."

"Be positive and it will," she said.

I know how Deon work and operated and he is bad about keeping his word but I had no choice but to hope he'd come through………at least for the sake of Kayla.

Well, we're here. Let's get this day started…..I thought to myself as we pulled up to the salon.

CHAPTER 3

"Lissa you had a message from the apartment complex. A lady named Mrs. Johnson wants you to call her."

"Okay, I hope I got this apartment Sonya," I said sincerely.

"You do Lissa. Put it all in God's hands and pray on it."

"I have prayed and hard, 'cause Momma D ain't playing," I said.

I picked up the phone and dialed the number that was left for me. As I dialed, I said a silent prayer, asking God to please have mercy on my situation. I was at my wit's-end and He was the only one who could help me right now.

"Hello, may I speak to Mrs. Johnson," I said when I heard the voice on the other line.

"Hi, this is Mrs. Johnson." The caller responded.

"This is Karlissa Thomas," I said, "you left a message for me to call you."

"Hi, Ms. Thomas, I was calling to let you know you can move in as soon as you bring me the security deposit and one month's rent. How soon can you have it?" Mrs. Johnson asked.

"What time do you close?" I inquired.

"We close at six o'clock," she answered me.

"See you at five o'clock," I said letting her know the deal was sealed. "Will I get my keys today?" I asked in an excited tone.

"You sure will," she concluded.

"Great," I nearly shouted, "I'll be there by five o'clock, see you then. Bye!" I said and ended our call.

"Sonya! Sonya, I got it, I got it!" I yelled out my excitement.

"Good! I'm so happy for you, girl!" she replied almost as happy as I was.

"How soon can you move in?" she asked, knowing I wouldn't waste time.

"If you take me to pick the keys up before five today, I can start moving right away!" I exclaimed.

"Well shoot, you ain't said nothin' but a word," she replied while laughing. "Let's get started!"

"Cool, let's do it," I shouted back.

I was so happy I could hardly wait to tell Momma D I had finally gotten my own place, just me and Kayla.

****

I made it to the rental office before five and just as promised, they gave me my keys and a quick walk thru the apartment. It was hood but it was mines. Now, I just needed to finish school so I could make some real money. Hopefully, I'd someday own my own beauty salon and call it *The Bougie Hair Boutique*. Yep, that all sounded good! But for now, I had to crawl before I could walk.

I rushed home to get all my stuff packed. Deon was on his way and I planned on giving him a key so he could check on us. The hood was dangerous and I had never lived up in the hood. I had hung in the hood and had cousins in the hood, but never had I lived in the hood. I was always dealing with a hood niggas. Something about loving a hood dude gave me a thrill! I'd always have a good time whenever I was out with one of them.

****

"There goes your daddy, Kayla," I said, hearing Deon when he arrived. "Knockin' like the damn police," I added in a sarcastic tone, "stop bangin' on the damn door, Deon!"

"Hey baby momma," he said in usual greeting.

"Ugggh! "Hey, baby daddy," I answered him back.

There go my girl, come here daddy baby," he called out to Kayla.

"Your damn twin is more like it," I said. The two of them looked so much alike there could never be denying her as his daughter.

"Here, please take these keys until Kayla and I get used to staying here."

"Cool, then I won't have to bang on the door," he said and laughed.

"But that don't mean come over anytime you get ready," I added.

"I got a key so that must mean that!" he replied with a devious smirk on his face. Nah, I ain't doing that. I'ma give you your privacy, but don't have no nigga in here, Lissa."

"How you gonna tell me who to have in my house?" I asked.

"You heard what I said."

"Whatever, Deon, anyway this shit is a hell hole. I'm in here for six months just long enough to build my rental history then I'm outta here," I said, meaning every word.

"Lissa, just stay to yourself, be cordial, and you'll be fine," Deon said offering his advice.

"I already know that," I replied.

"Now, what we gonna eat?" he asked.

"What y'all want?" I countered.

"Chinese is okay," he finally said. "Go 'head and call it in, by time I get there it will be ready. Oh, and just so you know, I'm spending the night," he sneakily said.

"Oh. Really?" I asked.

"I thought you knew?" He laughed.

"Nah, I didn't."

"Well, now you do," he said simply.

"Deon…..just go get our food," I said and laughed at his humor. "Sonya's calling me, go head, and I'll see you when you get back." He exited the house and I answered Sonya's call.

"Hey, Sonya, what's up, girl?" I answered.

"Hey Lissa, how you like it?" she asked inquiring about the apartment.

"Girl, it's cool. Just need a lot of stuff," I said.

"You'll get everything you need over time. You just gotta work hard," she added.

"Yeah……wha'chu doing?" I asked, changing the subject.

"Gettin' ready for work," she answered.

"Me too, I will see you tomorrow."

"Bye, Lissa." We said our goodbyes and ended the call.

****

Deon dropped me off at work then he took Kayla to his mom's house.

I walked in the salon and Sonya told me not to take my coat off. "We're going to the mall," she said.

"You don't have no clients?" I asked her surprisingly.

"Yeah, I have one coming in at one o'clock," she answered.

"Let's go, then," I said.

Sonya loved shopping. She'd spend thousands on purses and shoes. She would flip her clothes at the vintage shop when she got tired of them, if they were going out of style. She'd always find a way to let her clothes make money for her, and I couldn't be mad at that. *Gotta get with the hustle,* I'd say to myself.

I loved shopping with Sonya. We'd talk, have lunch and just have a ball together. But on this day, I didn't expect to have the conversation we'd had….

"Sonya your food looks good! What is that?" I asked.

"Indian food," she replied.

"Girl, you'll try anything," I said back in response.

"You have to be willing to try new things, Lissa," she said back, "how you gonna find out about the world if you don't?"

"You so right, but I rather stick with what I know," I said in a nonchalant tone.

Well, me, I'm a chance-taker. I'll try something at least once," she replied again.

"Good luck," I said and laughed.

"Girl, speaking of luck, I've been looking for a shop in Virginia, closer to my home."

"Why?" I asked, "You don't like *Talking Heads* no more?"

"Yea, but there's so much more out there to do," she informed me. "I'd like for you to go with me."

"How? I don't have a car and it's too far away. I gotta be able to get to Kayla quickly if anything happens," I said.

"That's true. So, what you gonna do if I take it, Lissa?"

"I'll have to find another shop to work for," I answered truthfully.

"Why don't you try where I first started, Four Stars."

"I never heard of it," I replied.

"Yeah, they may need shampoo girls. No Lissa you really you need to be on the floor. You're ready," she suggested.

"But, I don't have my license," I said, telling her what she already knew to be true.

"You can work under Dottie as apprentice. You got enough hours in school Lissa. I'll talk to the owner. She's good people," she offered.

"Let me think about it, Sonya," I said giving it some thought.

Well, just let me know when you ready," Sonya said. "Now let's get back to the shop.

CHAPTER 4

It didn't take long for me to get a new job, after calling half of the salons in the yellow pages. I got a job at *Angles* Beauty Salon as a shampoo Assistant.

I was doing well and learning a lot of new techniques. I had been doing everything to the client's hair except hot curling and styling the hair. I had to share my workload, every now and then with Jackie the owners cousin, Diamond.

Diamond was a college student. She'd come home some weekends and holidays. Jackie was the kind of person who showed favoritism and used you to her advantage, but, whenever family or friends came around she had no use for you.

One day, Jackie came over to me and said "I think you're ready for the floor.

I was so happy I had finally gotten promoted from shampoo assistant to stylist. I was doing everything except curling.

But the game still wasn't being played fair. Jackie would only give me clients who wanted finger waves, nothing else. And that was probably because it was something she couldn't do herself. She still used me as an assistant until she hired a new girl. Her name was Tammy.

Tammy was as far up Jackie's butt as she could go, and she'd jump, doing anything she asked. If Jackie wanted her shoes taken off, Tammy would do it, *and* rub her feet! Not me though. If it didn't have anything to do with hair, I didn't do it.

One day Jackie had Tammy doing everything that needed to be done in the shop. I was just basically sitting around doing nothing. It had gotten to the point that I couldn't even pay my bills anymore; because Tammy was getting all of the clients. I was a stylist now so there was no excuse for that. Every time a walk-in called or came in, she would never send them to me unless they wanted finger-waves.

Jackie wanted me to quit. She didn't wanna fire me because then she'd feel guilty, but I knew she really wanted Tammy doing all the hair. I was the one who had trained Tammy to be what she was. I got tired of the bullshit and finally did what she wanted, quit! So, back to the yellow pages I went, looking for another salon who would hire me.

CHAPTER 5

Sonya called to see how Kayla and I were doing. She asked if she could get Kayla for the weekend. "Sure you can, Sonya," I said with pleasure. I needed a break.

"Girl, how is work?" she asked.

"I hated it so I quit," I admitted.

"You quit? Why?" She wanted to know.

"Jackie never gave me any walk-ins and she always took them," I answered feeling annoyed at the mere thought.

"Lissa, you know better than that. Find another shop," she quickly added in. "You can do hair too good to give up. Call Dottie, I told her about you."

"You did?" I asked getting excited again.

"Yeah, and she's looking for your call. She's gonna look out for you, just call her," Sonya said.

"I will Sonya."

"Don't play, Lissa, I know you struggling with Kayla, and you not making no real money. You know what you doing though. Finish school, and get your license. But, in the meantime call Dottie. Dottie will help you. She knows I sent you," she repeated.

"Ok, I will. Deon, here, I gotta go. See you Saturday," I said before hanging up the phone.

"Who was that Lissa?" Deon asked.

"It was Sonya," I answered.

"What she up to?" he asked.

"Nothin'. She wants Kayla for the weekend."

"That's cool, you gonna let her go?" he asked.

"Probably so, I need a need a break anyway."

"Break to do what, Lissa?" Deon asked as if he were my father.

"Go out with my friends. You go out with your friends," I said aggravated at his questioning.

"Yeah I guess so." He agreed.

"I know so," I through back. "What brings you over anyway," I asked.

"I came to see my two favorite girls."

"Really?" I mocked him.

"Yeah, where's Kayla?"

"She's sleep so let her sleep."

"Well, in that case, I'm really here to see you." He smiled a crooked smile.

"I don't know what for," I said almost blushing.

"Let me show you," Deon said.

"Deon ain't nobody got time for your dumb shit."

"What dumb shit?" he asked as if he didn't already know.

"All them females you be messin' with."

"Man, you always messin' up the mood! I was trying to be romantic and here you go with the bullshit, Lissa!!"

"Deon, do you think you gonna have your cake and eat it too? Nah, it don't work like that," I said in a stern tone.

"Slim, don't make me fuck you up!" he said, getting angry.

"I can show you better than I can tell you," I hissed.

"Let me catch you, Lissa."

"You ain't gonna do shit!" I shouted at him.

"You'll see, Lissa, and come here!" he said, reaching out for my arms.

"Man, get off me and shut up, Deon…." I tried saying but he was already on me, "Damn, shut up…. Hmm…. damn that shit feel… oww right there!"

"Hmm you like that?" he asked.

" Don't stop. Oh, I ain't…. Damn your body beautiful, and you smell so good," he said out loud.

"Be quiet," I whispered, "you gonna wake Kayla up. Hmm…"

Deon would do this every time but his shit was so good. He knew what spots to touch and just how to touch it. If only he could keep his manhood to himself. He always said he'd never get married, and he would never be a one-woman man. Hey, with that being said, I had to do what I had to do. I had to find a new salon. I couldn't worry about what Deon was doing. I had to worry about Kayla and Lissa, making sure we had and we could survive out here, 'cause if not, we would be shit-out-of-luck! My Grandmother always said, *"God Bless the child that has its own"*. I was trying to keep my own.

CHAPTER 6

"Good Morning Four Stars!"

"Good Morning, may I speak to Mrs. Dottie?"

"Yes, this is Mrs. Dottie."

"My name is Karlissa. Sonya recommended me to you."

"Oh yeah, I been waiting for your call."

"Do you having any openings?"

"Yes, I do. Do you have a license?" she asked and my heart dropped.

"No, Mrs. Dottie, I'm still in school," I answered honestly.

"Not a problem. How many hours do you have so far?" she asked.

"I got 1000," I proudly stated.

"Oh, you're almost finished?" she asked right away.

"Yes, I am," I answered happily.

"Can you come in today?"

"Yes," I answered, "I sure can."

"Okay, you need to bring in your model and show me what you can do. I need to see you cut and style."

"Okay," I answered in agreement. "I'll be there within an hour.

"See you then, Karlissa," Mrs. Dottie replied.

"Bye, Mrs. Dottie." We ended our call.

I called my cousin to see if she would go with me to do the interview. "Hey Samiyah, can you go with me on this hair interview?"

"Yes, what I have to do?" she asked.

"I need to cut and curl your hair in front of her okay?"

"When Karlissa?" she asked.

"Now, can you take me?"

Yeah, be ready I am on my way, listen for the horn."

I hope I get this job. I can curl, but a short cut will be a problem, nothing beats a failure but a try. I thought. "Lord she's here already", I said to myself when I heard the sound of the car horn.

When we got to Mrs. Dottie's, it was very nice the salon. The workers all watched me. My nerves were so bad. *Lord, I don't need an audience,* I thought as I looked around.

"Where is your shampoo area?" I asked as I followed Mrs. Dottie through the salon.

"Come on sweetie, right this way," she said.

I shampooed Samiyah's hair and put her underneath the dryer. Me and Mrs. Dottie sat and talked while we waited. She asked me questions and gave me the do's and don'ts. Then I cut and styled Samiyah and Mrs. Dottie let me know she'd give me a call the following week. I said okay and thanked her.

****

Two days later, I got a call from Mrs. Dottie.

"Hello may I speak to Karlissa?"

"This is Karlissa."

"Hi, this is Mrs. Dottie, can you come in tomorrow to start and sign the contract?"

"Yes, I can," I answered happily.

"Also, I need you to come to Four Stars on the corner, not the one you came to for your interview."

"Okay see you tomorrow," I said. "Bye."

I was so happy I called Sonya. She was excited and said, "Let's go to dinner! I'll come get you and Kayla."

"Cool, I guess I will tell Deon later. Not that he really cares," I added. "Fuck it, I'll call him now. Hey, Deon!" I said when he answered.

"What's up baby mama?"

"You so ghetto."

"I got the job!!"

"Congrats, I'm happy for you!" he said.

"Thank you. Well let me go I got things to do. Pick Kayla up for me?" I asked.

"Nope, I got things to do too," he said.

"See how you do? Hello....?" The nigga hung up on me. "Fuck him!" I yelled out loud. "I'll get Sonya to take me around there to get her from Deon's mother's house. *That man is trifling! If it ain't about him, he don't want to do it.* I thought as I shook my head frustration.

****

So today was my first day at my new job and I was up and ready. I caught the bus and walked up to the door, and all eyes were on me.

"Hello, may I help you?"

"Yes, is Mrs. Dottie here?"

"Are you Karlissa?"

"Yes, I am."

"Okay, I'm Stacy. Your station is over there. You can go ahead and set up."

As I set up I looked around the salon, it looked like 1972, old as hell. It was Pepto Bismal pink with wall stations and carousels in the middle of the floor. Two shampoo bowls and old hair dryers sat against the wall. Ghetto! But hey, it was a start and I had a job.

Stacey was the first person I met and we instantly hit it off. She was real cool and the top stylist at the time. She had two assistants, Ralph and Shannon. Ralph was good at relaxing and coloring hair. He was very grumpy in the morning if he didn't have coffee or butter cookies. You got nothing but attitude from him. He was also a smoker and used the ashes from the cigarette to get the dye that was left on the client's skin, off.

Shannon was there to fill in where Ralph left off. Shampooing and wrapping, and sewing in weaves. Then there was Debbie; we called her Dizzy Debbie, but she could do a weave with her eyes closed. She had a lot of issues in her personal life.

I got my first client, and it was a wash and set. I was scared to death 'cause I really didn't know the workers and they were all quick to judge; if you messed a head up, they would help and correct it, and you and that person would split the money. After the client left they would talk about you and laugh at you. Once the laugh was over they would show you the correct way, or an easier way to do it.

I got a client who wanted a haircut. I couldn't cut, so I went to Stacey and asked could she do it for me. She said yes, but told me to watch and learn 'cause she couldn't keep doing my haircuts. I also had to pay for the cut. She asked if I had clippers and I told her no. "Well buy some when you get paid, but for now use mines," she offered.

"Okay," I accepted.

"Lissa, use the shampoo comb until you get good enough with the cutting, that way you won't have any holes or bald spots."

Ok I'll try it Stacey!! Lissa, see how easy that was? Yes, for you not for me. You'll get it. I hope so.

Stacey helped me for two weeks straight. I knew she was getting tired of me asking. This one particular day, I had gotten a client; usually Stacey would cut, and I would curl. It was time to cut so I called out to Stacey. "You ready?" I asked in my usual tone.

"Nah, I ain't doing it for you this time, you do it," she said. "If you fuck it up, I'll straighten it up."

"Do I have choice?" I whined liked a two year old.

"Nope, or give the client up,' she stated, plain and simply.

"So, I had no choice but to suck it up. I cut the woman's hair so good, everybody in the shop was shocked.

"I knew you could do it, Lissa!"

"I did do it, didn't I Stacey?" I asked, feeling a sense of accomplishment. Thank you for allowing me to watch you and learn from you. I can watch you from a far from now on."

"That's how I learn too, Lissa. Your cut was very good. You cut like a pro, girl! I'm going to call you *Star*."

"Why Star?" I asked curiously.

"That's a precision cut. You did that on the first go around. The name *Star* just fits you."

Thanks," I said sincerely and proudly.

Ever since that day, everyone in the salon had been calling me Star, except one person, Cindy. For some reason she felt as though I'd been hired to take her place. I had never seen her a day in my life. I didn't let her bring me down though; I was too happy. I was doing all my own cuts myself, and most importantly, I didn't have to share my money.

I was on a roll! I could do everything and anything! I had learned a lot being there in those three months. But.....I had also gained an enemy.

Cindy thought she was the bomb when it came to pencil curls. She thought I was there to replace her and she hated me. I had never done a thing to her. She would always say, *"I ain't callin' that bitch no Star, Stacey. Why not? Stacey would ask. That cut was banging! It was alright, Cindy insisted. Cindy you always hatin, Stacey would go on and on in my defense.*

One day Cindy had started her usual whispers of jealousy and like always, Stacey was there to speak up for me.

"You don't even know that girl and you hatin' on her like that, Cindy."

"I don't wanna know her, Stacey. You know they hired her to replace me."

Cindy that girl ain't here to replace you" Stacey said.

"How you know?"

"'Cause, she ain't," Stacey said once again, "but if that's what you wanna think then fuck it. That's on you. Just remember, Cindy, one day you gonna need her."

"I doubt that!" Cindy said in a harsh tone.

"Don't speak too soon, Cindy."

"Whatever, Stacey! Mark my work, I won't need her!"

****

Well, one day Cindy had an emergency. She had to leave to go get her son. She had a Jheri curl client waiting on her and nobody was available except for me.

"Stacey, can you take my client?" Cindy asked.

"Nope, I already got three. Give her to Star she don't have a client yet."

I ain't askin' that bitch nothin'," Cindy refused.

"So you rather risk losing your client by being mean?" Stacey asked dumbfound.

"Yup," Cindy replied with stank attitude.

"God don't like ugly and he ain't too fond of cute," Stacey shot at her with the sly remark.

"Alright, I'll ask her," she said giving in.

"Lissa, can you do my client?"

"Nope, I replied.

"Why not?" she asked, with a silly look on her face..

"One, you don't like me, and I ain't too fond of you. Two, I don't know how to do a Jheri curl."

It ain't that I don't like you Lissa. I thought you was here to replace me."

"Why would I replace you?"

"I don't know?"

"Tell me what I have to do?" I said feeling sorry for her although she'd mistreated me more than once.

"Apply the rearranger like a relaxer, let it sit until it's straight but don't let it over process, shampoo the hair, then roll it up with booster. Let it sit for twenty minutes. Then rinse with the rollers in then spray neutralizer and let it sit for twenty minutes under dryer. Rinse again, take the rollers out, spray activator on it, comb then she's finished." Cindy had given me step by step instructions.

"Can you at least help her if she has any questions Stacey?"

"Yes, this time I have my own clients."

'Thanks Star!!" Cindy shouted out with a huge smile on her face.

"Awww shit, she called me Star y'all!" I said smiling as big as she was.

"Star?"

"Yes, Mrs. Dottie," I replied.

"Do that client, time is money," she said.

"I'm doing her." I went on doing my job, and I became the Jheri Curl Queen. Nobody liked to do them so I took them over.

I didn't turn down any work. I was getting money, and I had two of the top stylist teaching me. I was on point! I was so into my making money I wasn't really paying Deon any attention. He was only my baby daddy, and word on the street was, he had hooked up with this young chick. I knew exactly who it was. Deon wouldn't admit it but I knew who she was.

Me and Kayla was out in Landover Mall getting her some Jordan's. On the way to the car, who do I spot? Monica and her girlfriend, driving Deon's other car. I walked up and asked, "Are you Deon's girlfriend?" She rolled the window up. That shit pissed me off so I kicked the window and said, "Bitch, let that window down! Are you his girlfriend?" She said yes and pulled off quickly. I laughed so hard. She was with her girlfriend but I was by myself. Kayla was in the car and only two years old at the time. They could have jumped me. Bitch knew better though! I would've caught her and fucked her up! Deon would have fucked her up too, so she did the right thing.

Deon wanna play? I thought deviously. *Let's see what CPS thinks about Monica being so young and Deon in his thirties. I don't think they'll like that one bit. Deon wanna play games, I'ma show him who invented Parker Brothers.* I laughed at my own silly humor.

****

"Hi, I was calling because I noticed this older guy who's always with this young girl, and I know it's not his child."

"Okay, Miss, can you give me the names?" The lady on the phone line asked.

"I'm not sure about the man's name but the young ladies name is Monica. She attends the High school around the corner," I said without a stutter or pause.

"What's the address, ma'am?" she asked, seeking the necessary information needed.

"3356 P Street SE Apt 6," I replied. I knew the address by heart and was happy I'd stored it in my mental rolodex.

"Okay, ma'am," she said as she took the info I'd given her, "someone will check it out."

"Thanks." It was done and the game was on, and I was in the lead. *Wanna play games*, I thought as I smiled a wicked smile, *checkmate mutherfuckers! He thought I wasn't gonna find out? Yeah, well, unfortunately for him, I did. Let me go home and get Kayla ready for bed.*

****

I got home and gave Kayla a bath. I wiped her down really good, so she'd be nice and clean. Suddenly, I heard this banging at the door. "Wait, Kayla, let's go see. I get to the door." I looked out the peep hole and it was Deon. "Why you banging at my door?" I asked already upset with him.

"Lissa, don't play with me. You know why!"

"Nah, I don't." I replied. I wasn't gonna say anything about the phone call unless I had to.

"Why you call them people and have them come to my house?" he asked surpringly.

"Your house? I don't know where you live so how could I have someone go to your house? You told me you still lived with your mother."

"I do." He lied.

"So what house you talkin' about?"

"Nothin'," he said.

"Nah…. ain't no nothin'. You come storm up here bangin' on my door, got my daughter scared and hugging me with the Kong foo grip! Hollerin' 'bout them people! Who is *them people,* Deon? And why was they at your house? The one you claim not to have that me and Kayla haven't been to yet!" I said sarcastically.

"Kayla been to my house," he said.

"Oh really, Kayla you been to daddy house?" I looked my daughter and asked.

"Yes with Grandma!" she shouted in delight. Kayla was clueless as to what was going on between her father and I. I was at least happy for that. She was too young to know everything, and although I'd had it with him, he was still and always would be, her father.

"No, where Monica lives," Kayla said letting the cat out of the bag. "Get the fuck out!"

"Lissa!! Lissa!" he shouted.

"I am done, Deon! I don't fuck with you! You be tryna carry the shit outta me and Kayla. It's all good though, we gonna be alright."

"Lissa, you ain't puttin' me out." Deon looked at me with fury in his eyes. He acted as though he was baffled by my reaction. I mean seriously, what did he expect from me? I had given him all the chances in the world and I was finally fed up with him and his BS.

"You gettin' outta here! We are done! Just take care of your daughter. You can see her when and how much you want, but me and you.... we done! I'ma give you some time to yourself and you can keep that shit 'cause I don't need it, Deon! Go be with your *Boo!" I said.* By now, my anger was at its boiling point.

"It's not over, Lissa," he insisted.

"I can show you better than I can tell you!" I replied with my arms folded over my chest.

"You better not have no niggas around my daughter!" he said, as if he were still in charge of *my life.*

"Bye Deon!"

"He got some nerve, but we gonna be alright," I said to my daughter. "Kayla, Mommie got you."

"Mommie got me?" she asked with a smile.

"Yes, Kayla. Mommie got you."

****

Mrs. Dottie was at the shop at eight o'clock and gone by three o'clock. One evening Stacey decided to get drinks and everybody pitched in. The first bottle of Alize was gone and we hadn't felt a thing.

"Star, you wanna get another bottle?" she asked me.

"Stacey, what about our clients?" I asked curiously.

"They won't know, we're not drunk," she replied.

"Alright," I agreed. She handed me $5.00.

By time we finished the second bottle we were so drunk. How we managed to finish up our clients and make it home, I'll never know.

The next morning I was up and ready for work. I loved that shop. Being a stylist, making money and living on my own was great! I kept using Deon for a ride to and from work. He'd have Kayla and me waiting at Ms. Anne's house 'til late in the evening. Ms. Anne would be pissed. She had no clue about Monica, until one day, I finally told her.

She told me to do whatever was best for me. "My son ain't no different from any other man. I love him dearly but wrong is wrong. Live your life and find someone that's gonna appreciate you," she said.

From that day forward Ms. Anne was an important part of my life. She became a mother figure to me, and anything she wanted or needed, I made sure she had. Kayla loved her to death and always wanted to be with her. It worked out well because Deon never had to come to my house. It was time for me to move on, get out, and meet people.

I had only been at Four Stars for 4 months. We had gotten one new worker, one return worker and had one leave. Mrs. Patsy couldn't take it anymore. It was too much drama for her. I knew how to stay out of it and mind my business. I had also gotten really close with two people, Kim and Lisa.

Lisa was my partner in crime. We were laid back and knew a lot of the same people. So, after work we'd sometimes hit the club. Ms. Mabel or Deon would keep Kayla. Lisa's mother or the kids' grandmother would have her kids.

One night we decided to go out. Lisa picked me up and we went to see Rare Essence. We had a ball. We ran into people we hadn't seen in years.

"Look, Star, there go Lonnie," she said.

"Oh, God here we go!" I said, laughing, "he gonna act a fool."

"Star!" he shouted out.

"Hey Lonnie"

"You still with that nigga Deon?"

"Why?" I asked, smiling hard.

"Man, I told you leave that old ass dude alone. He be messin' with this young girl in my court."

"What girl?" I asked.

"The young girl, Monica."

"Lonnie, that's probably a cousin," I said, knowing it was a complete lie.

"That's not that nigga cousin." Lonnie wasn't buying it.

"Don't be talking about my daughter father. You came to talk to me or to start shit?" I asked.

"Girl, you know I love you. I'm tellin' you 'cause I don't want your feelings hurt."

Lonnie, we not in relationship we just have a daughter together. I got caught up so I gotta take care of my responsibilities."

"I feel ya on that, just don't be no fool."

"I ain't." I said honestly.

"Star, you know I got you if nobody else don't. I was chasing you the whole nine months. What nigga chasing a chick trying to wife her and she pregnant? No nigga, none! If that ain't love I don't know what else is."

"That's true, Lonnie. Now give me a hug and a kiss you still love me?"

"You know I do!" he answered. "I'll see you after the club, Star."

"I rode with Lisa," I replied.

"Now you with me."

"Really, Lonnie?"

"Really, Star! Don't make me fuck you up! Don't do it love! Star you got jokes. When you hear *Before I Let Go*, and them lights come on, just be ready."

"Ok Lonnie, let me enjoy my drink."

"You heard me, Star?"

"Alright Lonnie!!"

"Star, what you going to do with him?" Lisa walked up and asked, nosily.

"Lisa, I don't know but did you hear what he told me?"

"No, Shawn was all in my damn ear soaking them up."

"Shawn!" I asked.

"Yeah Shawn."

"Wow, I didn't see him.

"You ain't miss nothing."

"What he say?" Lisa wanted to know.

"He confirmed just what Monica said," I replied.

"But you already knew that. You heard it from her."

"Deon ain't say it! A female will tell you anything if she wants your man. One thing about Deon he always had his own place. He has always been a flashy dresser. He almost forty years old and Deon not gonna keep living with his mother. I bet he got his own apartment and he moved Monica in there. He never told me in fear I may pop up. Fuck him and her, I ain't tripping. Just don't have my daughter around that bitch."

"I feel you, Star."

"Damn *Before I Let Go* just came on let's go before Lonnie spot us."

"He gonna kill you, Star."

"I got him. I gotta go to work in the morning. I ain't fooling with Lonnie."

Got to work and somebody had been stealing supplies. Dottie was heated. She'd always sent me and Stacey, or Lisa to get the supplies. Me and Stacey together, spelled trouble. This time she sent me alone. When I got back all hell had broken lose. We had bag and trunk check. Dottie knew who was doing the stealing but kept it under wraps 'til the time was just right.

Saturday came and I had no babysitter. Kayla went to work with me. It was 6:30am.

We were on the bus headed to the salon when Kayla said, "Ma, something on fire, look at the fire trucks."

"Yea baby something is. It's time to get off the bus so we'll see."

We got off the bus and walked towards the shop. Kayla said, "Mommy the shop on fire!" and we started running.

When we got down there Kim was outside with Dottie. I asked what happened. Dottie said she got a call that the shop was on fire and to get down there quick.

"Damn," I said, "Hey Kim."

"Hi, Star and Kayla," she greeted me back.

"What's wrong?" she asked when she noticed the sad look on Kayla face. "Where am I gonna work?" She replied when reality sat in.

"My shop burned down, Kim," Kayla said.

We all laughed then cried; the baby had more sense than we did. We laughed to keep from crying. The good thing was there was a Four Stars 1 and 2. So, all of us went up to Black Radiance to work.

****

Eighteen women worked in one shop, two to a station and some had three. Whoever didn't have a client, moved and let the person who had one work. This was survival of the fittest; blood sweat and tears. You had four top stylists in one shop, and others who were trying to get on their level. You mess up, you get knocked off, can't take the pressure, you roll out. That's what happened.

In four months everyone had their own station. We had one new worker, Janelle. Janelle wasn't a team player so she quickly fell off. By being a team player you took a lot of shit. She had a hard time dealing with Dottie.

Dottie was as sweet as could be, and looked out for you. But, there was two things Dottie loved to do, that was eat and gamble. Every day at three o'clock Dottie was out the door, on her way to eat and play Bingo. She even went out of town to Bingo, and it was by any means necessary. Most of the means came from shop money. By Friday she was working us like Hebrew slaves to get the money back so she could pay us. That's the part Janelle couldn't deal with; not getting paid on time, so she rolled out. That's what most of the stylist did who worked for Dottie. We might not have gotten along or even liked each other but we had each other's back.

One Saturday, this chick decided she wanted to get her hair done, but didn't wanna pay. We were not having that. She came in said, "Good morning, my name is Missy, and I have a appointment with Stacey."

"Ok, sign in and her assistant will get you started."

After going to the back she got her hair relaxed, shampooed, wrapped, cut and styled. Stacey said, "Missy, your hair is sixty five dollars."

"I'm gonna pay you next Monday, I don't have it," Missy answered in a snotty tone.

"Are you for real? Did you discuss this with Dottie?" Stacey asked.

"No I thought I had to talk to you about my payment."

"No, you need to go talk to Dottie. Why you wait 'til I finish your hair to say you can't pay 'til next Monday? Go to Dottie, she's at the desk. Tell her about your payment."

"Ok, hi I'm back," Missy said to Dottie.

"Oh, your hair looks nice," Dottie said noticing she was done.

"Yes it does, Dottie. Thanks."

"Did she give you the ticket?"

"Yes, here is my ticket."

"Ok, it's sixty five dollars ma'am."

"I will pay it next Monday."

"Come again, what you say?"

"I want to pay you next Monday."

"Missy, you have to pay when service is rendered."

"Well, I don't have it."

"Can you borrow it from someone and have them bring it to you."

"No, I gotta pay you next Monday."

"No, we gonna have to shampoo your hair. We can't let you do that its stealing."

"Wash my hair?"

"Yes, shampoo your hair."

"I'm not stealing. I told you I would pay you next Monday."

"Missy,, please step to the back and get your hair shampooed, or I'm gonna call the police."

"You not gonna shampoo my hair, and why you lock the doors?"

"'Cause you stealing from us. Missy, won't you please get your hair shampooed?"

"Look you old bitch, I told you I will pay you next Monday."

While Dottie was talking to the client, Stacey told us what went down. When Dottie gave us the signal we lit her ass up with the water bottle. She started swinging and ran into the bathroom and wouldn't come out. We called her all kinds of names and yelled, *come out you can't hide.*

Nikki and Kandi got to arguing. Nikki swung, and before I could break it up Kandi grabbed my stove to slap her with it. *Shit, there goes my stove.* I thought.

"Star, I will buy you another one! This bitch act like I was the only one spraying water!" Kandi yelled.

"Nikki you saw Dottie signal Lock down, and you knew what would happen. My ass wet too! We all wet. But I'm soaked and wet, Kandi. Nikki you walked over here just when it started to go down, so yea, you gonna be soaked too."

"Look y'all chill out! The police are here, or are y'all going with her?"

"She wrong, Star. I ain't apologizing it was all of us."

"Nikki, let it go, you ain't dying. Now you won't have to take a bath tonight," I said.

"Star don't be funny," she said.

"I ain't, I'm so serious. Oh shit they got her."

"Ma'am, we gonna read you your rights. We're arresting you for failure to pay, which is considered a petty larceny charge, along with disorderly conduct," the arresting officer said.

"But officer, they wet me up," Missy complained.

"You refused to pay, Ma'am," the officer said before turning to leave.
"You ladies have nice day."

"Thanks, you do the same." A few of us replied.

"Man, that lady was tripping, y'all! I bet she won't do that again Stacey said!"

"I bet she won't either. Nikki, come here."

"Yes, Dottie?"

"Why was you acting a fool? You heard and saw what was going on but you had to be extra."

"No, Mrs. Dottie I was soaked."

"I'm soaked too but you know how it goes."

"There needs to be a better way."

"Oh really, you right. Now go home. I'll see you on next Saturday."

"Why you walking me."

"'Cause you was disorderly in my salon."

"I got soaked and slapped with a stove and I get walked?"

"You started it. There's a better way right?"

"Sure is, I quit."

"Good, your services are no longer needed. Remove all items and while you doing that I will cash you out the fifty dollars you made me all week."

"Mrs. Dottie thank you, I ain't even gonna fuss."

"Nice knowing y'all and good riddens."

"You leaving for real Nikki?"

"Yes Star. I can do better than this. I am far more talented."

"Good luck. I will miss you."

"Once I leave, you not even gonna remember me. But I loved working with you."

That's not true. I wish you luck."

"Go ahead. Dottie's calling you.

"Star, take this client."

"Okay. Hi my name is Star, how can I help you today."

"Shampoo and Wrap."

"Can you go in the back with my assistant? He will take care of you. You can set your bag by my station."

"Ma'am, I am Gerald. You can come with me. Star, I will bring her back when she's ready to be curled."

"Cool, I will be on the other side. Stacey guess what? What? Stacey, why she just give me a client? She don't want me to leave. I'm gonna do this lady so fast. I am tired. Too much went on today. Nikki quit 'cause the lady didn't want to pay, what's next?"

"Nothing I hope. I can't take no more."

"Me either, Stacey"

I have finished my client. Now I am gonna pack up. Then I am outta here.

"Damn, she calling me."

"Go see what she wants."

"I hope not another client. Yes Dottie?"

"What are you doing?"

"Talking to Stacey and cleaning up to go home."

"Well, I just wanna let you know I can't give you all your pay."

"Why not?"

"We didn't make enough. Here is your envelope."

"Dottie, I got daycare and bills to pay."

"Star, I have the rest of your money but it's in change ."

"What?"

"Yes change."

"Dottie, just give me the change. *I can't believe this shit she just paid me in nickels and dimes.* I thought to myself. "Bye Dottie, see you on Tuesday. *Who the hell does this? Pay you in change? Dottie that's who.*

"So what she want Star?"

"You not gonna believe this."

"What?"

"She paid half of my money in change."

"What?"

"Yes, change!"

"Star you lying!"

"Look!"

"Oh shit!"

"I swear she better have all my money."

"I don't think so. I think she split it between the both of us."

"Lord, help her. I'm gone girl."

"See you next week, Star, be careful."

"I will. Shit I got a rock in a sock. I'm well protected with all these nickels and pennies!"

"Girl bye! You fool!"

"Bye Stacey!"

As soon as me and Kayla got to sleep we heard shots. "Mommie!! Mommie!! What was that?" Kayla said aloud. It got louder and closer, just kept going *pop, pop, pop!* Oh my God! It was a shootout! I grabbed Kayla. She cried as we crawled to the bathroom, closer to the door. All of a sudden we heard this loud screech, and the hall on the floor lit up then the shooting stopped. We waited for about ten minutes. I peeked out the door and my living room was so bright. I had no furniture yet but my curtains were up. I finally came all the way out of the bathroom when I heard the sirens coming. A car was inches from coming thru my living room window.

The next morning I looked for apartments. I ain't never lived in the hood and today was my last day in the hood. Five days later I got a call that I had gotten the apartment and I could move in. I moved in the next day and was out of the other apartment by the end of the month.

Deon wouldn't be getting a key to this one. He was with Monica so he didn't need a key anyway. But you know he was ignorant and cut a fool.

Around the second month while walking from the store I met this dude named Steve. He was quiet and a little strange, but I liked him. We hit it off well. We had been dating for a year....

One day as he was leaving and Deon showed up. He acted an ass. He got out of his car and headed to my door, about to knock, as it opened. Steve spoke and said, "Hi, how you doing?" as he said bye to me. Deon stood, looking. Steve went outside to warm his car up but I thought he had left.

Deon said, "I got something for Kayla in the car." He walked out, flashing his gun so Steve could see it. Steve laughed when he walked passed. He blew his horn and waved good-bye, laughing. I guess Deon thought that was gonna scare Steve off, not!

Steve was a straight hood nigga, with a lot of strange ways. Steve and I dated for three years. He was in and out of jail. The last time I said fuck it, changed my number and moved on.

Some years later, I heard Steve got married and was arrested for being a rapist. I guess Deon felt something wasn't right about him. *Glad he never asked me to marry him.*

On Tuesday morning I arrived at work. My first client was a Jheri Curl so Pam went to get the reformer out from the back. We had three more curls coming in. Now, just last week I bought two jars from the Beauty supply store. Now Dottie was pissed. Cindy came in hollering good morning. Dottie sent me and Stacey to get supplies, and Tony's to get food.

Stacey said, "Hey look at them Cadillac's Star, let's go look Stacey."

"Ok."

We pulled in the lot and got out of the car and listened to what the sale's man had to say. I walked off looking at the Toyota and then walked back over to where Stacey was. She handed me some keys and said, "Here, let's go Star."

I said, "Okay," and went to get inside of the car.

"No, we leaving that car and taking this one, Stacey said in a matter-a-fact tone."

"Stacey, whose car is that?"

"This the new one," she said.

"For real? Oh shit, we was rollin'"

We got back and Stacey told Dottie to come out and look. "That's a nice Cadillac."

"You like it Dottie?"

"Yeah, Stacey it's nice. Is it yours?"

"I traded in your Cadillac for this one Dottie."

"Stacey if you and Star don't get your ass back to that car lot and get my Cadillac I'm gonna kill one with the other."

"Stacey I thought you said she knew."

"Well she know now."

"Girl I am gonna kill you!!"

"Star take her ass back up there and y'all bring my damn car back! Don't go nowhere else!"

"Now we gotta hear this shit all day!"

I was finally back from getting Dottie's car and done with my client. It was almost six o'clock. Cindy was going out the door and Dottie said we were gonna do a bag check. Cindy gave her the bag then left. When we got ready to leave we gave her the bag.

"If y'all two don't get away from me after what y'all did today," Dottie said and chuckled. I hurried up and left.

The next morning Cindy had three clients waiting on her, but she hadn't arrived. She called and said she was on her way. Dottie told her she'd send someone to pick her up. She sent Lisa and Stacey.

Cindy wasn't dressed when they got there. They went inside and *bingo!* All of the missing hair supplies were there. Now Dottie got on our nerves but we loved her to death. Stacey went off and called Dottie. Dottie told her not to say anything and to bring her to work.

Dottie let her finish her three clients and write her ticket out for the day. She gave her the money back she earned, and Cindy said, "Today's not Saturday, Dottie."

"I know that, Cindy," Dottie said, "but your services are no longer needed."

We fell out laughing and Cindy cut up a fool. But she knew not to act simple so she packed her things and left. That was the end of Cindy and the supply count stayed on point from that day on.

Now Reece always wanted me to call him a *she*, but to get under his skin I would always say *he*. We argued day and night. But Reece was cool people 'til she scared the shit out of my child.

Kayla was raised in the shop. She was a shop baby which meant she spent a lot of time in the shop. She was very spoiled and everybody loved her and wanted to pinch her fat cheeks.

One day Reece decided he was going to do his wave in the shop. Kayla was so scared all you saw were tears running down her face. See Kayla was very quiet and would sit and read books. You'd never know she was there. Today was looking sad and I had to ask why. "Kayla, what's wrong?" I asked.

"He ugly!" she replied. I was laughing so hard, he was mad as hell. That's when the argument started.

Reece ran to Dottie and said, "You gonna tell Star to stop disrespecting me!" You see Reece was Dottie's gambling partner so she took up for him. But today Dottie was holding in her laugh. She was just as crazy as we were. Dottie just looked at him and didn't say a word cause she would have busted out laughing. So I walked in the back and he right on my heels.

"You gonna respect me," Reece said.

I turned and said, "God made you a *he* and that is how I will address you."

Dottie hollered, "Star!!"

"Yes!" I answered.

"Come to the desk!" she called out.

I get up front, she giggling. "Star, call him a *she* that if that's what he wishes to be called. I refused so Dottie walked my ass for a couple of days, for not following the rules. It hurt my pockets like hell too! Dottie knew how to make it hurt.

I went home to chill. I was washing clothes and the phone rang.

"Hello?"

"What the fuck you doing arguing with transvestites?"

I came to your job looking for you and Lisa told me what happened.

He scared Kayla."

"That's still dude, why you aint call me?"

"Lonnie it ain't that serious."

"Come scoop me."

"From where?"

"The ugly people house."

"Give me minutes."

"Nah, come now!!"

"Wait a minute! Hello? This nigga hung up on me" *Let me get my shoes....good thing Kayla gone with her Grandmother til Sunday. Lonnie always tripping.*

"What took you so long?"

"Lonnie, I had to put clothes on."

"Next time move faster, go 'head with that."

"Where you need to go?"

"Up your house."

"Alright, I ain't dropping you back off."

"Did I ask you too?"

"You smart ass."

"Nah, I am just messing with you, plus I wanna take a nap."

"Alright, cool I am washing clothes any way."

While I cleaned and mopped he took a nap and a shower and fixed something to eat. Then,

Lonnie friend came to pick him up. I went to clean Kayla's room and put the clothes away, and the phone rang again.

"Hello?"

"What you doing?"

"Cleaning, Deon…why?"

"Lonnie is dead!"

"What you say?"

"You heard me, that nigga Lonnie is dead," and he hung up.

I dropped the phone and started shaking. Screaming, hollering throwing things. I couldn't believe it we been thru thick and thin together. Once I got myself together I called Lisa.

"Hello?"

"Lonnie is dead!"

She said, "What you say?"

"Lonnie dead!"

"You okay?"

I guess so, but he just left here three hours ago. What happened Lisa asked. I don't know yet. Let me call around to see what happened. I called my friend that lived in his court. She said someone shot him in the back of his head over twenty dollars in a crap game, by the ugly people house. All I could do was cry.

Two days later I got myself together and called his family. I asked if they needed his clothes or anything. They said they did but they never came to get them. I smelled his shirt every day because it still had his scent on it.

It was the day of the funeral and me and Lisa were dressed in a black and white linen pant. We walked in the funeral and all eyes were on us. We were the best dressed in the church while everybody else was dressed like they had just come off the porch.

We got to the casket and they had Lonnie dressed the way he dressed in the hood, old sweat pants and a sweatshirt. I didn't understand, but it wasn't my place. But I knew if he was here he would've went the hell off!! We left the funeral and got back to the shop to finish our day.

It was Saturday and very busy. It was Easter time. Stacey's sister was getting her hair done. It was late in the evening and she was like y'all want something to drink? We all hollered yeah. Alright, I'm gonna call my homies to come down here so we can get some drinks. In thirty minutes these dudes came asking for Nina. We called her to the front and when she came, I went back to my station. Wouldn't you know my spritz was missin'! *Damn you can't have shit!*

"Who got my spritz?"

"I got it girl. I didn't feel like walking to my station."

"Girl, next time warn me. I'm walking round thinking somebody stole my spritz. Why he keep looking at me?"

"Star I don't know but it looks like he saying come here."

"Lisa I ain't going out there. Both of them saying come here."

"Star if you go, I'll go. No we don't know them. I think they are with Nina. Oh Lord here they come.

"Hi, my name is Charles, what's yours?"

"My name is Star."

"You think I can take you out?"

"Charles I don't know you."

I am trying to get to know you by asking you out to eat or movies?"

"Maybe."

"Put your number in my phone, Star."

"Here you go."

"Alright I'll hit you up later."

"Cool."

"Star they seem cool Lisa said."

"Yeah, probably to chill with, ain't nothing wrong with having friends Lisa."

"Nope sure aint."

As the day went on, I noticed Dottie looking a little sad and red in the face. Whenever Dottie sat at the desk, rubbing her hands, there was a problem.

"Dotties what's wrong?"

"Come here, Star. Can you stay late 'cause I don't have enough money to pay everybody."

"You did this to me last week not again this week, I can't keep doing this. I gotta get my child."

"I understand that, Star. But we got clients they have to be done."

"Dottie you always call me and Stacey to stay no one else and it's not fair." Ask Koko or Moni sometimes.

"You're my top girls. I know y'all get them in and out."

"This the last time don't ask me next week cause the answer will be no."

"I will send you the next client. Tell Stacey to come here."

"OK. Stacey Dottie wants you."

"What she want?"

"What she always want."

"For me to stay late?"

"You guessed it."

"I don't mind today. I don't have shit to do and I need some money anyway."

As time went on things got horrible, but we worked through it and stuck together. Dottie sat at the desk just smiling.

"Dottie, it's cold in here," I said.

"Star, go check the base boards to see if they warm."

'Nope they not," I replied again.

"Is the water hot?" Dottie asked knowing my answer would be no.

"Nope."

"Let it run longer," she insisted.

"I did it's still not hot."

"Dottie when the last time you paid the gas bill?

I don't know Star.

"No wonder we blowing smoke at each other."

Dottie ain't paid the gas bill."

"Lord, Lisa doing a perm."

"Warn her cause that water ice cold."

Lisa the water is cold in the back, no hot water!"

"Did you let it run?"

"Sure did!"

"That damn Dottie ain't pay the gas bill."

"Oh well gotta rinse her in cold water. No wonder it's so cold in here!"

"Yeah, no gas. I'm bringing a heater tomorrow."

"Star, we all gonna have pneumonia fooling with Dottie!"

"Sure is!"

By the next month the ceiling was leaking in bathroom. You had to use an umbrella to use the bathroom. The electricity got cut off so we ran a cord from the car lot to the salon to get electricity. People would call the board on us but some how we still passed. We did this for the next two years. The clients didn't care and they still continued to come and to get their hair done. One day Dottie called a meeting to let us know the salon might be closing because she owed back rent. We were all pissed.

"How do you owe back rent and we make all this money? And you can't keep gas, electric or water, now the rent?" Stacey asked infuriated.

"Yes, Stacey we just not making enough," Dottie said.

"No, you just doing too much bingo." Dottie rubbed her legs, as tears ran down her eyes. I don't care about no tears. "You gotta stop. When you get it, pay it. How we gonna work? This how we pay our bills. And how much is it three thousand? That's two months and next week makes another fifteen hundred added on to that three thousand. So what's the outcome Dottie?" Stacey continued.

"What y'all plan to do? I don't know. I guess we need to find somewhere else to work."

"No, Stacey I will figure it out."

"We',ll see but in the mean time we all will be looking for a job. Come on y'all."

We all went and sat on my side. "Damn every week it's something. What we going to do? Any ideas? Why don't we all put in and pay it. Then we will surely have somewhere to work."

"Star that sounds good but is Dottie going keep paying it?"

"Look we collect the money, give it to Mrs. Kim and we still got a place to work!" Y'all in?"

"Yeah I am in, we all in."

By Saturday we had 3000 dollars. Everybody gave up their pay check and the rent got paid. Six months later, we were under new management because they opened Four Stars back up. Dottie was sent down there to manage. Koko took over, but it was still in horrible condition. Nadina ran the desk. Koko had everybody do booth rent to make things easy, but the workers started to quit because the salon was in horrible condition. So Koko was like we're gonna have to close the doors on New Year's Eve. I think that was the saddest day of our lives. We all went our separate ways.

I left and went to Hair Solution's beauty Salon and the same thing happened there that happened at Four Stars. It closed down. One of my coworkers died and the other became ill. The owner decided to close the shop for good, taking her business to her home and some years later she died.

In the two years I was there I opened my own salon and called it Bougie Chic's Hair Boutique. Bougie Chic's has been pumping ever since and we are a full service spa. We have a clothing line, adult toys and makeup line. My chairs are fuscha pink and my walls are black and white with a fuscha stripes. My stations are black with fuscha stripes. I have ten stylists.

We specialized in weaves, eyelashes and eyebrows. I had my own personal section for my clients. I had two assistances, Brandi and Kayla. Kayla came in during the afternoon because she was in her second year of college. Yes, Kayla was grown now and she thought she could get over just because she was my daughter. But, she soon found out I don't mix personal and business. Kayla's my baby, but I learned fast because she would try to get over on you.

"Kayla, how many clients we have today?"

"Dawn wanna get her hair done.

"We have ten clients today, Star."

"Dawn can get squeezed in at lunch," Star said.

"Don't have me here all night, Star," Dawn butted in.

"Girl you gonna have to be patient and wait, or just come another day. I can't be putting you in front of people cause you my friend Dawn."

"Star you know we going out I need to look snatch. Eric gonna be there you know he been trying holler for a minute."

"Oh yeah, Spring Fling Party? Those parties be on point, Star! They be having them free Patron and 1800 shots free for ladies all night."

"Exactly!! Dawn you know Eric just wanna hit right?"

"Shit, that's cool too. I wanna know what he working with anyway."

"Bitch you a ho!"

"Nah I just want what I want. I got to be on point myself. Lisa what you gonna wear?"

"I bought an all-black dress and some Jimmy Choo strap-up-the-leg sandals."

"Damn, girl you ready!"

"Bitch, I stay ready!"

"Well, I hope you be ready tonight and not still in this shop Star."

"Dawn, I'll be ready. Matter-of-fact my last client is at four."

"Dawn, the problem gonna be Star."

"Why me, Lisa?"

"You don't know how to cut off Star."

"That's where you wrong, my last is at six."

"I bet."

"Dawn, you make sure you be back by 1 o' clock, so my assistant will be able to get you in and out."

"Star I'ma roll 'cause I need you to be ready when I get back. Make sure Kayla is here, you know I love me some Kayla."

"Get out, she don't love your ass."

"I beg to differ."

"You just be ready, Star! When I get back them clients better be gone!"

"Bye Dawn, they will, you just hurry up back here so I can get you done."

"Lisa, I don't even have anything to wear tonight I really don't feel like it but Dawn will have a fit if I don't go. Plus I already got my tickets. My hair ain't even done I gotta get it shampooed and wrapped. Let me hurry up."

"Yes 'cause you look a hot mess, Star."

"Ain't that some shit?"

"Nah, it's the truth Star."

"Real cute."

"Well what you gonna do about an outfit?"

"I might have to send Kayla to the mall and have her face-time me in the store."

"Sounds like a good Idea."

"Yep, Lisa I think that is what I will do."

"Kayla, I need you to go to the mall."

"You buyin' me something?"

"Dang, why you can't go just because I need you to?"

"Alright Ma, I just want a shirt for the party tonight."

"What party Kayla?"

"We gonna hit this girl party at the club. ByB gonna be there."

"Okay, find me something good. I'll get you a shirt if it's off the chain. I'll add some jeans too. I need a banging dress and shoes."

"What time you need me to go?"

"Now, but you need to be back by twelve thirty."

"Why?"

'Cause Dawn will be back by then. Kayla you know you the only one she lets touch her hair."

"Ma, I know. That'll buy my shoes, auntie Dawn tips good."

"Girl, get out of here."

Kayla knew just what I liked; my jeans to fit and my tops cute. Shoe game crazy.

"I love some boots with a heel. They bring out the sexy in me. I'm sure as hell gonna be sexy that night. Really," I said.

It wasn't a game with these dudes. If you had a cute face, big ass and nice size breasts, they'd be on you. They be hollering, *Shawty what your name is!"*

"Star, do my hair girl! You a fool. I gotta pick my kids up."

"Girl, I ain't said nothin' but the truth."

"Face-time me when you get in the store, Kayla."

"I will, Ma. I'm taking your car."

"Now, I'ma kill her if she tear my shit up. Then, I'll be driving hers."

'Girl you got that girl so spoiled."

'I know Ms. Betty. It's always been me and her."

"Lisa, don't act like that 'cause you sure ain't know better."

"I ain't said nothin' 'cause I know how my sons are."

"Why we do that?" I said to no one in particular.

"I don't know. It's too late now they grown."

"I hope their spouses can handle it when that time comes."

"I know right Star."

"Oh well, better them than me."

"Star you terrible."

"I know," she said and laughed.

****

Star had finally finished up at the shop. She went home and changed her clothes to get ready for the party.

"Again her motherly instinct kicked in and she asked, "Kayla, where you going tonight?" she asked her daughter.

"Ma, I'm grown," Kayla replied.

"I'm gonna ask you again…where you going tonight?"

"I am going to see ByB at the club," Kayla answered this time, "I told you that earlier when you asked me."

"Who going with you?"

"Dang, Ma! Jasmine and Bree are going with me."

"Alright, y'all be safe. You look cute, and I love that shirt."

"Thanks Ma. It's the one I got from the mall," Kayla said.

"No drinking and driving either!" Star added.

"I won't, Ma. See you later!" Kayla called out.

"Kayla I love my dress, Karlee said.

"I got taste!" Kayla turned and yelled back.

I need to get dressed, she thought to herself. *Dang, this dress Kayla got me is bangin'! An all red form fitted dress with the heels to match. I guess I'll push the white Benz tonight. This just may be my night.* Dawn tryna get Eric I think I'll see what's up with his friend Kadoe. Kadoe was chocolate and fine. He had to be at least six feet tall with a body like the Hulk. *I wonder if he's still with that chick Tasha.... It don't matter 'cause when he sees me in this dress it's a done deal. Oh my, it's getting late, let me go.*

"Who is calling me?" she asked herself aloud. She saw that it was Bink calling, so picked up, "Hey, Bink what's up?"

"You know Kayla up here?" he asked.

"Yeah her, Jasmine and Bree are all together," Lissa replied.

"What? You doing security up there tonight?" she asked.

"Nah, just here 'til my shift start."

"Okay, Bink."

"I got her Star, I'll keep my eyes on her for you."

"Make sure she safe, Bink."

"She good," he reiterated.

"Kayla, who with you, just y'all three?"

"Yeah Bink.

"Go ahead, I'll be gone in little bit," Bink said.

"How they get to bust!" someone hollered?

"Bitch, mind your business," Kayla hollered.

"Bitch this is my business, you got in front of me!"

"Alright, cut it out! Them my folks you gonna get in," Bink said. "It's enough niggas to go around."

"Damn shorty, they carried you!" somebody hollered."

"My name ain't shorty, its Sheri. Ain't nobody carried me!"

"You know you next so what's the problem. You mad or nah?" Kayla said

"Never that Ms. Kayla and bitch you don't know me!"

"Oh, but I do. Really, you keep talking you gonna wish you didn't know me," Kayla said. "I see you all talk no bite, Sheri.

Before I knew it, I just stole the shit out this bitch.

"Did she just hit me?" Sheri said?

I stole her ass again. Before I knew it, four chicks came out of nowhere and we were all fighting. Bink's big ass picked me and Bree up in one swoop, and threw us up against the wall, Jasmine was behind us.

They put Sheri and her crew out. But not before I got one more punch in. "Bitch every time I see you, we gonna fight!" Kayla hollered.

"I'm always ready. And I'ma get you bitch," Sheri said.

"I'm real easy to find Kayla hollered."

Bink made us leave and it wasn't even twelve o'clock.

"Go home, Kayla, they not gonna let y'all in now since I'm leaving, to go do security at a party."

"Alright, you'll probably see my mom there so please don't tell her what happened here," Kayla pleaded with Bink.

"I'm not, but stop fighting so much Kayla," Bink said.

"I was minding my business, Bink," Kayla said her defense.

"True, but sometimes you gotta ignore people Kayla."

"I know… you're right. I gotta be the bigger person, right?" she stated.

"Exactly, bye Kayla and friends," Bink called out.

"Bye Bink!" they all yelled back.

Even though Bink had told the girls to go home, they already had plans of their own. The night was still young and they wanted to show off their new hair-dos and outfits as well. No way were they headed in so soon.

Not only that, but Kayla wasn't finished with Sheri. She was hoping to run into her and keep the promise she'd made. She had plans on stomping her really good next go 'round.

Little did Kayla know, the night would take a turn for the worst, and it would be one neither she, nor her mother would soon forget.....

To be continued….

Part 2 coming soon!!!!

Made in the USA
Columbia, SC
04 May 2025

57499840R10059